Jack and the Beanstalk

Illustrated by Ed Parker

This edition published in 2002.

Library of Congress Catalog Card Number: 78-18072

ISBN 0-8167-7505-2

Printed in the United States of America.

15 14 13 12 11 10 9 8

Once upon a time there was a widow who was very poor. All she had was a lazy son named Jack, and an old cow named Milky White. Every day, they would milk the cow and take the milk to market to get enough money to buy food. But one day, there was no milk to sell.

"There is only one thing left to do," cried the widow. "We will have to sell Milky White!"

So Jack led the cow down the road toward the market. On the way, he met a strange little man who said, "Good morning, Jack! And where are you going with your cow?"

"I'm going to sell her at the market," replied Jack.

"Just so!" said the strange little man. "But do you know how many beans make five?"

Now Jack was as sharp as a needle, so he quickly replied, "Two in each hand and one in my mouth!"

"Just so!" said the man. Then he took five strange beans from his pocket, and said, "And here they are! Now, because you're so sharp, I'll trade you these beans for your cow. Mind you, they're magic beans. If you plant them, they'll grow right up into the sky."

Well, Jack knew a good bargain when he heard it. So he traded Milky White for the five magic beans. When he got home, his mother asked how much he had sold the cow for. "You'll never guess," replied Jack. "Look! Five magic beans!"

"Beans!" cried his mother. "Oh, you silly lad." Then she threw the beans out the window and sent Jack to bed without supper.

When he awoke in the morning, Jack saw something
outside his window. It was a huge green beanstalk,
growing right up into the sky. So the man had told the
truth after all! Jack began to climb the beanstalk at once.

He climbed, and he climbed, and he climbed, and finally he reached the sky. There, he found a long road that led to an enormous house. And on the front steps was a huge woman.

"Good morning," said Jack. "Might I have some breakfast?"

"Breakfast!" cried the woman. "If you stay here, you'll *be* breakfast! My husband is a giant who likes to broil little boys—and eat them on toast!"

But Jack was so hungry that the giant's wife took
him into the kitchen and gave him something to eat.
Before he had finished, Jack heard the giant's footsteps.
Thump, thump, thump! The whole house seemed to shake!

"Quick!" said the wife. "Hide in here." And she pushed Jack into the oven. Just then, the giant stomped into the kitchen, roaring:

> Fee fi fo fum,
> I smell the blood of an Englishman.
> Be he alive or be he dead,
> I'll grind his bones to make my bread!

But the giant's wife said, "You just smell the scraps of the boy you had for yesterday's dinner."

When the giant had finished his breakfast, he took some bags of gold from a big chest. He set them on the table, and began counting. Before long, his head began to nod, and soon the whole house shook with the sound of his snoring.

Jack crept out of the oven, seized one of the bags of gold, and fled to the beanstalk. He dropped the bag down to his mother's garden, and climbed down after it. "See, mother!" he said. "They were magic beans after all."

And so, for a time, they were able to live comfortably. They bought whatever they needed with the giant's gold. But at last the bag was empty, and Jack decided to go up the beanstalk again. So one morning, he climbed, and he climbed, and he climbed to the top of the beanstalk. Then he went down the road to the big house, where the giant's wife stood at the door. Jack went right up to her and said, "Good morning! Might I have a bite to eat?"

"Go away," said the woman. "If you stay here, my husband will take a bite of *you*!" Then she said, "Say— you look like a boy who came here once before. That same day, a bag of gold disappeared!"

"Maybe I could tell you something about that," replied Jack. "But right now, I'm too hungry to talk about

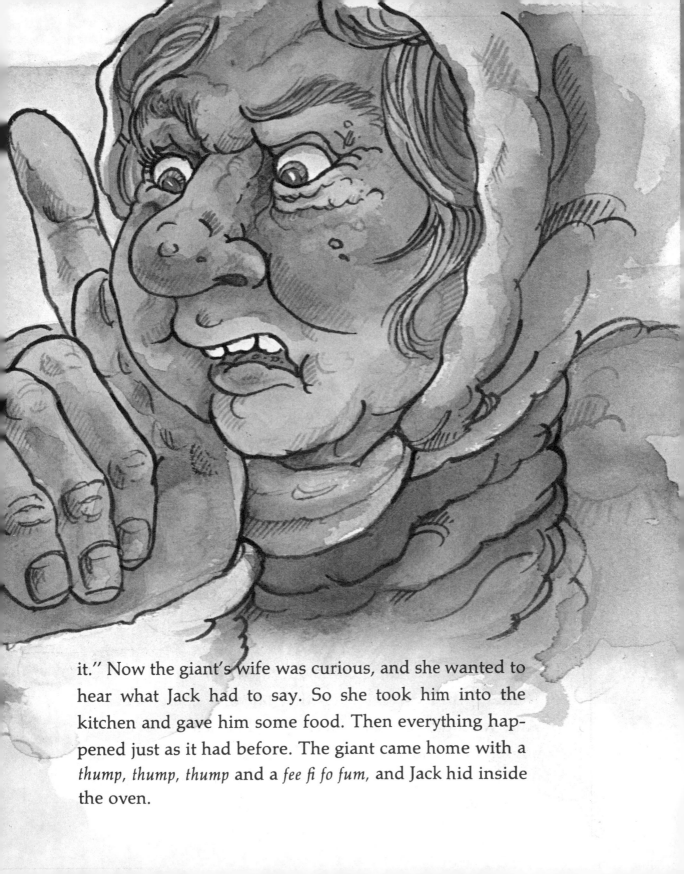

it." Now the giant's wife was curious, and she wanted to hear what Jack had to say. So she took him into the kitchen and gave him some food. Then everything happened just as it had before. The giant came home with a *thump, thump, thump* and a *fee fi fo fum,* and Jack hid inside the oven.

Then, after the giant had eaten his breakfast, he roared, "Bring me my hen that lays the golden eggs!" And whenever he said "Lay," the hen laid a beautiful golden egg! Soon the giant fell fast asleep. Jack grabbed the hen, ran to the beanstalk, and climbed down as fast as he could.

When he got home, he showed the hen to his mother. And whenever he said "Lay," the hen laid a golden egg. So now Jack and his mother always had plenty of money.

But one day, Jack grew restless. So he climbed the beanstalk again. This time, he hid near the giant's house until the giant's wife came out to fetch some water. Then he slipped into the kitchen and hid in a big copper pot.

When the giant came in, he roared, "Fee fi fo fum, I smell the blood of an Englishman!"

"It must be that boy who stole your gold and your hen," cried the giant's wife. "If it is, he'll be hiding in the oven." They pulled open the oven door, but of course, Jack wasn't there. So the giant sat down to breakfast. And when he had finished, he called for his golden harp.

"Sing!" he said, and the harp began to sing. The beautiful songs made the giant sleepy, and before long, he was snoring as loud as thunder.

Jack crept out of the copper pot and snatched the golden harp. But the harp cried out, "Master! Master!" and the giant awoke in a rage. Straight to the beanstalk ran Jack, with the giant close behind. Jack jumped onto the beanstalk and started climbing down.

At first, the giant was afraid to get onto the wobbly beanstalk. But when he heard the harp cry out again, he started down after Jack. The beanstalk began to swing back and forth under the giant's weight.

By this time, Jack could see his mother's house. He
cried out, "Mother! Bring an axe!" And his mother came
running with the axe. Jack jumped to the ground, seized
the axe, and swung it at the beanstalk. Then he swung it
again. And this time, the giant came crashing down and
the beanstalk came toppling after.

Jack showed his mother the golden harp, and whenever they said "Play," the harp played beautiful music
for them. They grew rich from the hen's golden eggs.
Jack even married a princess, and they all lived happily
ever after.